The
Great Pet Sale

Mick Inkpen

Orchard Books : New York

"EVERYTHING MUST GO!"
said the sign on the pet shop
window.

In the window was a rat.
I looked at him. Half of his
whiskers were missing.
"I'm a bargain!"
called the rat
through the glass.

"I'm only 1 cent!
Choose me!"

Inside the shop there was

a tiny terrapin for 2 cents,

a turtle for 3 cents,
and a tortoise—
a great big one—
for 4 cents.

3¢

2¢

"I'm sure you wouldn't like
one of THOSE!" said the rat.
"But you'd like me . . .

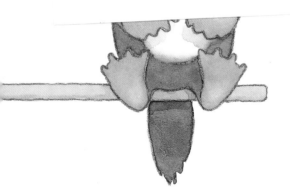

THINGS
BEGINNING
WITH "P"

5¢

EACH

On the perch were
"THINGS BEGINNING
WITH P."
A parrot,
a pelican,
a penguin,
a puffin,
and a platypus.

All 5 cents each.

"Oh, you don't want
anything beginning
with P!" said the rat.
"R! . . . R is what
you want!
R for Ratty!"

Behind a plastic rock was
a salamander for 6 cents,
a skink for 7 cents,
and a gecko for 8 cents.

"Which one is which?"
I said.
"Nobody knows!
Nobody cares!" said
the rat.
"Sausages on legs!
You don't want
one of THOSE!"

9¢
FOR THE PAIR

The next two animals were
"**9**¢ FOR THE PAIR."
    "Who wants a koala that
doesn't like leaves?" said the rat.
"Or an anteater that won't
eat its ant?
    I'm not fussy!
    I'll eat . . .

...ANYTHING!"

ASSORTED
LITTLE
BROWN
CREATURES

In the cardboard box were
"ASSORTED LITTLE BROWN CREATURES,
EVERYTHING FOR 10¢."

"Boring! Boring! Boring!"
said the rat. "I'm not boring!
Look! I can stand on one leg!"
And he did.

At the back of the shop, we came
to a big door.

"What's in there?" I said.

"Oh, just a dragon," said the rat.

"There's no such thing," I said.

"Then you won't want one,
will you!" said the rat.

I unlocked the door.
It *was* a dragon. A great
big Komodo dragon

for 25 cents!

I counted my money.

$1.00 exactly.

It was just enough
to buy the rat . . .

E
INK
    Inkpen, Mick
    The great pet sale   3/99